A Beginning-to-Read Book

Dear Dragon's Fun With Shapes

by Margaret Hillert
Illustrated by David Schimmell

NORWOOD HOUSE PRESS

DEAR CAREGIVER, The *Beginning-to-Read* series is a carefully written collection of classic readers you may remember from your own childhood. Each book features text comprised of common sight words to provide your child ample practice reading the words that appear most frequently in written text. The many additional details in the pictures enhance the story and offer the opportunity for you to help your child expand oral language and develop comprehension.

Begin by reading the story to your child, followed by letting him or her read familiar words and soon your child will be able to read the story independently. At each step of the way, be sure to praise your reader's efforts to build his or her confidence as an independent reader. Discuss the pictures and encourage your child to make connections between the story and his or her own life. At the end of the story, you will find reading activities and a word list that will help your child practice and strengthen beginning reading skills.

Above all, the most important part of the reading experience is to have fun and enjoy it!

Shannon Cannon

Shannon Cannon,
Literacy Consultant

Norwood House Press • P.O. Box 316598 • Chicago, Illinois 60631
For more information about Norwood House Press please visit our website at
www.norwoodhousepress.com or call 866-565-2900.

LIBRARY OF CONGRESS CATALOGING-IN-PUBLICATION DATA
 Hillert, Margaret.
  Dear dragon's fun with shapes / by Margaret Hillert, illustrated by David Schimmell.
   p. cm. -- (A Beginning-to-Read Book)
  Summary: "A boy and his pet dragon look at shapes such as squares, circles and triangles and then go outside to find shapes in nature and objects"--Provided by publisher.
  ISBN 978-1-59953-544-9 (library ed. : alk. paper) -- ISBN 978-1-60357-410-5 (ebook) [1. Dragons--Fiction 2. Shape--Fiction] I. Schimmell, David, ill. II. Title.
  PZ7.H558Delf 2012
  [E]--dc23

                              2012012628

Manufactured in the United States of America in North Mankato, Minnesota.
             206N—082012

Cookies, cookies.
I like to work with you Mother.
I like to help make cookies.

Cookies have shapes.
This one is a circle.

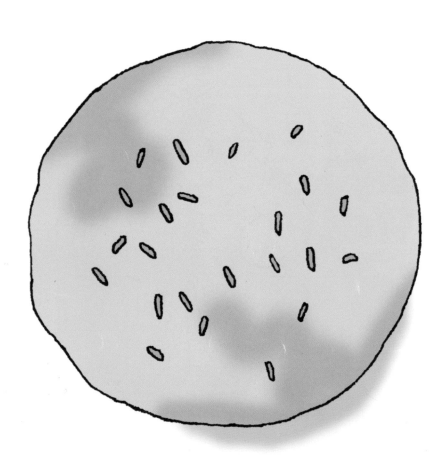

The red cookie has
a triangle shape.

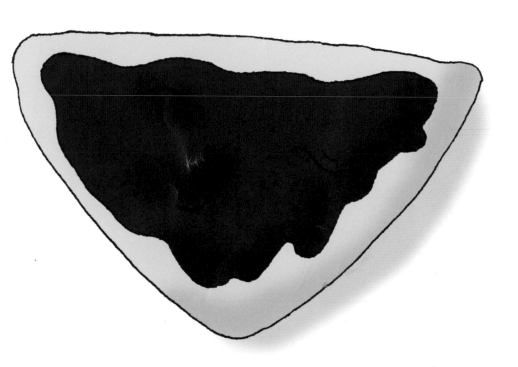

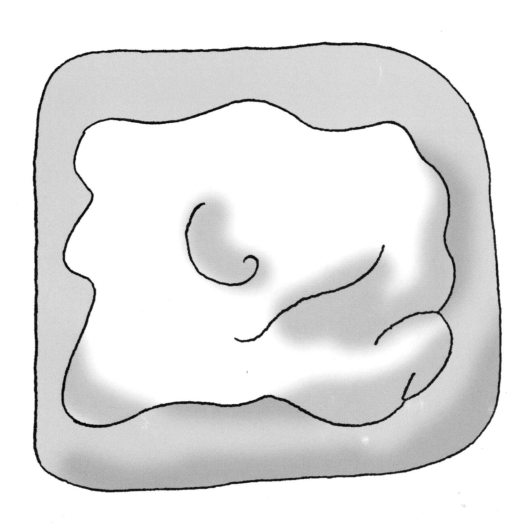

This one is a square.

A dragon has a lot of shapes!

Mother, I see a man
at the door.
Look. Look.

I have something
for you.

You are good to me.
This makes me happy.

Look Mother.
This is a square box.
Can you guess what is in it?

I will guess there are toys in the box.

Oh, boy!
Oh, boy!
What fun this will be!
See what I can make!

This is like the triangle I play at school.

Now I want to go out and look for shapes.

Here. Here.
Come and eat some circles and triangles.
Then you can go out.

Yes, Mother.
That looks good.

I am on two circles!
And look up there— a triangle.

I can make this circle work.

Look at it go.

And I can walk on these squares.

This little circle is a good help to me.

Look up there.
That looks like a circle too.
We have to go in now.

Here you are with me.
And here I am with you.
Oh, what a good day, dear dragon.

The following activities support the findings of the National Reading Panel that determined the most effective components for reading instruction are: Phonemic Awareness, Phonics, Vocabulary, Fluency, and Text Comprehension.

Phonemic Awareness: The /s/ sound

Oddity Task: Say the /s/ sound for your child. Say the following words aloud. Ask your child to say the word that does not end with the /s/ sound in the following word groups:

bus, yes, yet	gas, gab, kiss	cab, bats, cabs	miss, mess, mix
us, play, plus	this, less, fast	set, loss, toss	past, pass, pats

Phonics: The letter Ss

1. Demonstrate how to form the letters **S** and **s** for your child.

2. Have your child practice writing **S** and **s** at least three times each.

3. Ask your child to point to the words in the book that start with the letter **s**.

4. Write down the following words and ask your child to circle the letter **s** in each word:

see	sit	is	Sam	say	was
saw	bears	shapes	kiss	something	she
basket	pass	star	said	house	sun

Vocabulary: Concept Words

1. Write the following words on separate pieces of paper:

   Triangle   Square   Circle   Oval   Rectangle

2. Read the words to your child and ask him or her to draw the shapes on separate pieces of paper.

3. Mix the words up randomly and ask your child to match their drawings to the written words.

Fluency: Shared Reading

1. Reread the story to your child at least two more times while your child tracks the print by running a finger under the words as they are read. Ask your child to read the words he or she knows with you.

2. Reread the story taking turns, alternating readers between sentences or pages.

Text Comprehension: Discussion Time

1. Ask your child to retell the sequence of events in the story.

2. To check comprehension, ask your child the following questions:

   - What is the boy baking with his mother?

   - Who is at the door?

   - What is in the box the boy opens?

   - What instrument does the boy play at school?

   - What is your favorite shape? Why?

WORD LIST

Dear Dragon's Fun With Shapes uses the 76 words listed below.
The 4 words bolded below represent the name of shapes and serve as an introduction to new vocabulary, while the other 72 are pre-primer. You may wish to write the words on index cards and use them to help your child build automatic word recognition. Regular practice with these words will enhance your child's fluency in reading connected text.

a	eat	like	red	**triangle(s)**
am		little		two
and	for	look(s)	school	
are	fun	lot	see	up
at			**shape(s)**	
	go	make(s)	some	walk
be	good	man	someone	want
box	guess	me	something	we
boy		mother	**square(s)**	what
	happy			who
can	has	now	that	will
circle(s)	have		the	with
come	help	of	then	work
cookie(s)	here	oh	there	
		on	these	yes
day	I	one	this	you
dear	in	out	to	
door	is		too	
dragon	it	play	toys	

ABOUT THE AUTHOR Margaret Hillert has written over 80 books for children who are just learning to read. Her books have been translated into many different languages and over a million children throughout the world have read her books. She first started writing poetry as a child and has continued to write for children and adults throughout her life. A first grade teacher for 34 years, Margaret is now retired from teaching and lives in Michigan where she likes to write, take walks in the morning, and care for her three cats.

Photograph by Glenna Washburn

ABOUT THE ADVISER Shannon Cannon contributed the activities pages that appear in this book. Shannon serves as a literacy consultant and provides staff development to help improve reading instruction. She is a frequent presenter at educational conferences and workshops. Prior to this she worked as an elementary school teacher and as president of a curriculum publishing company.